An I Can Read Book™

STUART L

Stuart at the Library

story by Susan Hill

pictures by Lydia Halverson

HarperCollins*Publishers*

HarperCollins®, 🎬®, and I Can Read Book® are
trademarks of HarperCollins Publishers Inc.

Stuart at the Library
™ and © 2001 by Columbia Pictures Industries, Inc. All Rights Reserved.
Story by Susan Hill
Illustrations by Lydia Halverson
Printed in the U.S.A. All rights reserved.
www.harperchildrens.com

Library of Congress Cataloging-in-Publication Data
Hill, Susan.
Stuart at the library / by Susan Hill ; pictures by Lydia Halverson.
    p.   cm. (An I can read book)
Summary: At first Stuart is afraid of Bookworm the library owl, but they become friends
when Stuart says he will help Bookworm learn to read.
    ISBN 0-06-029538-4 — ISBN 0-06-029632-1 (lib. bdg.) — ISBN 0-06-444303-5 (pbk.)
    [1. Mice—Fiction.   2. Cats—Fiction.   3. Books and reading—Fiction.]   I. Halverson,
Lydia, ill.   II. Title.   III. Series.
PZ7.H5574 Ss   2001   00-066364
[E]—dc21

❖
First Edition

STUART LITTLE™

Stuart at the Library

Late one afternoon

Stuart Little went to the library.

"Do you have any books

for someone like me?"

he asked the librarian.

"How about *Mice Are Nice*,"

she said. "Third floor."

"Thanks," said Stuart.

"Is that a stuffed owl?" he asked.

6

"No, no. This is Bookworm.

He is our library owl.

We let him live here

because he loves books so much,"

said the librarian.

Bookworm opened one eye
and stared at Stuart.

"Owls and I don't usually get along,"
said Stuart.

"Don't worry," said the librarian.

"He usually sleeps

during library hours."

"Well, thanks for the help,"

Stuart said to the librarian.

Stuart found the book.

"I'll just read a little bit to see

if I want to borrow it," Stuart said.

Stuart began to read.

Soon he was lost in the story.

Then he fell asleep!

Something woke Stuart.

"I must have slept
past closing time," said Stuart.

"Indeed you have," said a voice.

"Bookworm? Is that you?"

Stuart asked.

The big owl flew out of the shadows.

"It is I," said the owl.

"Oh dear," Stuart said,
and he began to back away.
"Never fear," said Bookworm.
"I've already had my dinner.
Besides, I want to read my books,
not chase mice."

"I love to read, too!" said Stuart.

"What's your favorite book?"

"There have been so many,"
Bookworm said.

"*Whoo* can pick just one?"

"Pick a few, then!" said Stuart.

"Hmmm, yes, well . . ."

Bookworm pointed

to the closest book on the shelf.

"I am quite fond of this one,"

he said.

"This book?" Stuart asked.

"Yes. It is a work of art
that has great meaning to me,"
said Bookworm.

Stuart looked at the book.

"You like *Lawn Care for Dummies*?"

"Is that the title?"

Bookworm said.

"Can't you read it?" asked Stuart.

"Well, no," said Bookworm.

"And no one else can find out.

I'm afraid I'll have to eat you

after all!"

Bookworm dived for Stuart.

Stuart ran!

Bookworm chased Stuart
down the hall, around the corner,
and down the stairs.
Stuart could not escape.

Bookworm landed on top of him.

"Please, Bookworm,

let me go!" Stuart cried.

"I am sorry, my bookish friend.

My secret must stop with you!"

"Wait!" cried Stuart.

"You said you weren't hungry!"

"I'm not," said Bookworm,

"but I will be sent away

if the librarian finds out

I can't read.

I am a library owl, after all."

"I promise I won't tell anyone,"

said Stuart.

"Maybe I can help you."

"I don't need help from a mouse,"

said Bookworm.

"Now, you'd better go.

Shoo! Shoo!"

Soon Stuart went back to the library.

Bookworm opened one eye and asked,

"What are you doing here?"

"I want to help you read," said Stuart.

"Well, don't bother me,"

said Bookworm.

"Let me sleep."

"When you wake up," said Stuart,

"here are some other books

you might like."

"Let me see those," said Bookworm.

"What is this one about?"

"It's about a very smart owl

who finds out

it's never too late to learn,"

said Stuart.

"Well, if you insist," said Bookworm.

"Why don't you start?"

"You bet!" said Stuart.

And the two new friends

began to read together.